by Donna D. Cooner, Ed.D. illus. by Kim Simons

To Gary, one of the blessings I always count first.

—DDC

To my parents.

—KS

Count Your Blessings

Based on the words from the refrain of the hymn, "Count Your Blessings" by Johnson Oatman, Jr.
Music by Edwin O. Excell

Managing Editor: Laura Minchew
Project Editor: Beverly Phillips

Library of Congress Cataloging-in-Publication Data.

Cooner, Donna D. (Donna Danell)
Count your blessings/by Donna Cooner; illustrated by Kim Simons.
p. cm.
"Word kids!"
ISBN 0–8499–1199–0
1. Children—Prayer-books and devotions—English. 2. God—Goodness—Juvenile literature. 3. Creation—Juvenile literature.
[1. Prayer-books and devotions. 2. Counting.]
I. Simons, Kim, 1955– ill. II. Title.
BV4870.C643 1995
242'.62—dc20

94–45281
CIP
AC

Count your blessings,
Name them one by one.

Count your blessings,
See what God has done.

5
6
7
8
9
10

One, two—
Big hugs for you.

Three, four—
A winning score.

4

Five, six—
Colors to mix.

Seven, eight—
Pink roller skates.

Nine, ten—
A toothless grin.

Count your blessings,
Name them one by one.
Count your blessings,
See what God has done.

One, two—
Trips to the zoo.

Three, four—
Shells on the shore.

Five, six—
Clowns doing tricks.

Seven, eight—
A birthday cake.

Nine, ten—
A special friend.

Count your blessings,
Name them one by one.
Count your blessings,
See what God has done.